the BOSS BABY

For Jerry and Nancy, my parents

SIMON AND SCHUSTER
First published in Great Britain in 2011 by Simon and Schuster UK Ltd
1st Floor, 222 Gray's Inn Road, London, WC1X 8HB
A CBS Company

Originally published in 2010 by Beach Lane Books,
an imprint of Simon and Schuster Children's Publishing Division, New York

A CIP catalogue record for this book is available from the British Library upon request

HB ISBN: 978 0 85707 351 8
PB ISBN: 978 0 85707 312 9

Printed in China

10 9 8 7 6 5 4 3 2 1

the Boss Baby

AS HIMSELF!

by Marla Frazee

SIMON AND SCHUSTER

From the moment the baby arrived,

it was obvious that he was the boss.

He put Mum and Dad on a round-the-clock schedule, with no time off.

And then he set up his office right smack-dab in the middle of the house.

He made demands.
Many, many demands.

And he was quite
particular.

If things
weren't done
to his immediate
satisfaction,

he had a fit.

He conducted meetings.

Lots

and lots

and *lots* of meetings,

many in the
middle of
the night.

The funky thing was, he never, ever said
a single word that made any sense at all.

But that didn't stop him.

As boss, he was entitled to plenty of perks.

There was the lounge.

The spa.

And the executive gym.

There were drinks
made to order,
24/7.

And, of course,
the private jet.

Then one day, all activity ground to a halt.

The boss surveyed his surroundings,

eyeballed his workers, and frowned.

He called a meeting.

His staff did not respond.

He called and called and called. Nothing.

The boss's usual demands were not getting their usual results.

It was time to try something
completely out of the box.

Ma-ma? Da-da?

Wow. That worked.

For the first time since his arrival,
the boss baby was pleased.

But only momentarily.

He had to get back to the office ASAP.

There was still a business to run here.

And make no mistake...

he was the boss of it.